The Velveteen Rabbit

Adapted from the story by Margery Williams

Illustrated by Judith Sutton

A GOLDEN BOOK • NEW YORK

Golden Books Publishing Company, Inc., Racine, Wisconsin 53404

There was once a velveteen rabbit. In the beginning he was really splendid. His coat was brown and white, and his ears were lined with pink sateen. On Christmas morning he waited in the Boy's stocking.

For a least two hours the Boy loved him, and then in the excitement of looking at all the new presents, the Velveteen Rabbit was forgotten.

For a long time the Velveteen Rabbit lived in the toy cupboard in the nursery. Some of the more expensive toys snubbed him. The mechanical toys were very superior and pretended they were real.

Only the Skin Horse was kind to the Velveteen
Rabbit. The Skin Horse was very wise and had lived
longer in the nursery than any of the other toys.

"What is REAL?" the Rabbit asked the Skin Horse
one day. "Does it mean having things that buzz inside
you and a stick-out handle?"

"Real isn't how you are made," said the Skin Horse. "It's a thing that happens to you. When a child REALLY loves you, then you become Real."

"I suppose you are REAL?" asked the Rabbit.

"The Boy's uncle made me Real many years ago," the Skin Horse said. "Once you are Real, it lasts for always."

The Rabbit sighed. He thought it would be a long time before this magic thing called Real happened to him.

One evening the Boy couldn't find the toy dog that always slept with him. Nana gave him the Velveteen Rabbit instead.

That night, and for many nights after, the Velveteen Rabbit slept in the Boy's bed.

At first the Rabbit found it rather uncomfortable. Then he grew to like it, for the Boy made nice tunnels for him under the bedclothes. The Boy said they were like the burrows real rabbits lived in. When the Boy dropped off to sleep, the Rabbit would snuggle down and dream.

So time went on. The little Rabbit was so
happy, he never noticed how his velveteen
fur was getting shabbier, his tail was
coming unsewn, and the pink was rubbing
off his nose.

Once the Rabbit was left out on the lawn until long after dusk. Nana had to go and look for him because the Boy couldn't sleep.

"Fancy all that fuss for a toy!" said Nana.

"He isn't a toy," the Boy said. "He's REAL!"

When the little Rabbit heard that, he was happy, for he knew that what the Skin Horse had said was true at last. He was Real! The Boy himself had said so.

One summer evening the Rabbit saw
two strange beings creep out of the woods.
They were rabbits like himself. They must
have been very well made, for their seams
didn't show, and they changed shape when
they moved.

"Why don't you get up and play with us?" one of them asked.

"I don't feel like it," said the Velveteen Rabbit.

"Can you hop on your hind legs?" asked the other.

"I don't want to," answered the Velveteen Rabbit.

One of the rabbits came very close and sniffed.
"He hasn't got any hind legs!" the furry
rabbit called out. "And he doesn't smell right!
He isn't a rabbit at all! He isn't real!"

"I *am* Real!" said the little Rabbit. "The Boy said so!"

Just then the Boy ran past. With a flash of white, the two strange rabbits disappeared.

For a long time the little Rabbit sat still, hoping the two rabbits would come back. But they never returned.

Then one day the Boy grew very ill. It was
a long, weary time, for the Boy was too ill
to play. But the little Rabbit snuggled down
patiently and looked forward to the time
when they would play like they used to.

At last the Boy got better. The doctor ordered that all the toys the Boy had played with be burned. So the little Rabbit was carried out to the garden.

He thought of the Skin Horse and all that he had said. Of what use was it to be loved and become Real if it all ended like this? And a tear, a real tear, trickled down his nose and fell to the ground.

Then a strange thing happened. Where the tear had fallen, a flower grew. And out of that flower stepped a fairy. She kissed the Rabbit on his velveteen nose.

"Little Rabbit, don't you know who I am?" she asked.

It seemed to the Rabbit that he had seen her face before.

"I am the nursery magic Fairy," she said. "I take care of all the playthings that children have loved. When the children don't need them anymore, I turn them into Real."

"Wasn't I Real before?" asked the little Rabbit.

"You were Real to the Boy," the Fairy said, "because he loved you. Now you shall be Real to everyone."

The Fairy took the rabbit and flew to the woods. There, in a clearing, the wild rabbits danced, but when they saw the Fairy, they stopped and stared at her.

"I've brought you a new playmate," the Fairy told them. "Be kind to him, for he is going to live with you forever!"

The little Rabbit sat still for a moment. He did not know that when the Fairy had kissed him, she had changed him altogether. Just then something tickled his nose, and he lifted his leg to scratch it.

And he found that he actually had hind legs!
Instead of velveteen, he had brown fur, and his
ears twitched.

The Rabbit gave one leap, and his joy was so
great, he went jumping sideways and whirling
around as the others did.

He was a Real Rabbit at last!

In the Spring, the Boy went out to play. Two rabbits crept up and peeped at him. One of them had strange markings under his fur, as though long ago he had been stuffed.

The Boy thought, "Why he looks just like my old Bunny!"

But he never knew that it really was his own Bunny, who had come back to look at the child who had first helped him to be Real.